MW01043589

Mexico

by Barbara Saffer

Consultant:
Dr. Susan Schroeder
France V. Scholes Professor of
Colonial Latin American History
Stone Center for Latin American Studies
Tulane University
New Orleans, Louisiana

Bridgestone Books
an imprint of Capstone Press
Mankato, Minnesota

Bridgestone Books are published by Capstone Press
151 Good Counsel Drive, P.O. Box 669, Mankato, Minnesota 56002
http://www.capstone-press.com

Library of Congress Cataloging-in-Publication Data
Saffer, Barbara.
    Mexico/by Barbara Saffer.
    p. cm.—(Countries and cultures)
    Includes bibliographical references and index.
    ISBN 0-7368-0772-1
    1. Mexico—Juvenile literature. [1. Mexico.] I. Title. II. Countries and
cultures (Mankato, MN.)
F1208.5 .S194 2002
972—dc21   00-009718

Summary: An introduction to the geography, history, economy, culture,
    and people of Mexico.

Editorial Credits
Martha E. H. Rustad, Connie R. Colwell, and Leah K. Pockrandt, editors;
    Lois Wallentine, product planning editor; Heather Kindseth, designer;
    Heidi Meyer, illustrator; Katy Kudela, photo researcher

Photo Credits
Betty Crowell, 31; Capstone Press/Gary Sundermeyer, 51; Carol Kitman, 24, 42,
50, 55; Corbis, cover; Digital Stock, 1 (left, middle), 45, 56, 63; Max & Bea
Hunn/The Image Finder, 52; Michele Burgess, 16; North Wind Picture Archives,
27, 28; PhotoDisc, Inc., 1 (right), 18; Photo Network/Howard Folsom, cover;
Photo Network/bachmann, 46; Photo Network/Jeff Greenberg, 49; Reuters/Bob
Strong/Archive Photos, 15; Reuters/Jeff Mitchell/Archive Photos, 32; Trip Photo
Library/Ask Images, 39; Unicorn/Jeff Greenberg, 34; Visuals Unlimited, 13;
Visuals Unlimited/David S. Kerr-Jimenez, 23; Visuals Unlimited/Francis and
Donna Caldwell, 8; Visuals Unlimited/LINK, 4; Robin Karpan, 21

Artistic Effects
Capstone Press; Digital Stock; PhotoDisc, Inc.

Reading Consultant:
Dr. Robert Miller, Professor of Special Education, Minnesota State University,
Mankato

1 2 3 4 5 6 07 06 05 04 03 02

Contents

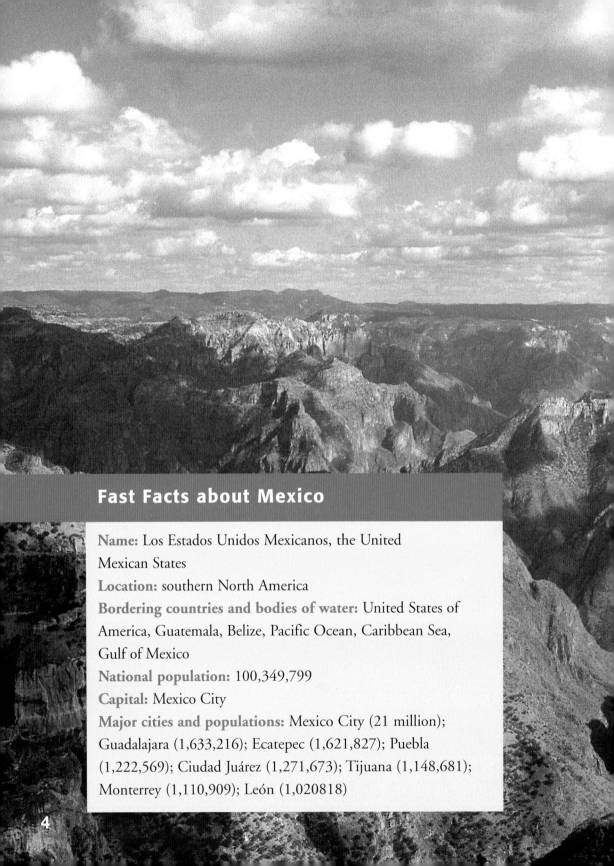

Fast Facts about Mexico

Name: Los Estados Unidos Mexicanos, the United Mexican States

Location: southern North America

Bordering countries and bodies of water: United States of America, Guatemala, Belize, Pacific Ocean, Caribbean Sea, Gulf of Mexico

National population: 100,349,799

Capital: Mexico City

Major cities and populations: Mexico City (21 million); Guadalajara (1,633,216); Ecatepec (1,621,827); Puebla (1,222,569); Ciudad Juárez (1,271,673); Tijuana (1,148,681); Monterrey (1,110,909); León (1,020818)

Explore Mexico

Mexico's Barancas del Cobre, or Copper Canyons, make up the largest canyon system in the world. Covering more than 20,000 square miles (52,000 square kilometers), the system is four times larger than the Grand Canyon in Arizona. Four of the canyons are at least 5,900 feet (1,800 meters) deep. More than 900 miles (1,400 kilometers) long altogether, the canyons are 1 mile (1.6 kilometers) wide in places.

Visitors to the Copper Canyons can tour small towns and view native wildlife. The small village of Batopilas is located at the bottom of the Batopilas Canyon. Cowboys and the native Tarahumaras people live in Batopilas. Black bears, mountain lions, and foxes wander through the canyons as eagles, hawks, and macaws soar above the landscape.

◀ Copper Canyons, the largest canyon system in the world, stretch north to south through west central Mexico. Rivers carved the deep canyons thousands of years ago.

A Land of Contrasts

The Copper Canyons system is only one of the many amazing sights in Mexico. The country's variety of landscapes—from mountains and deserts to beaches and forests—is just one reason the country has earned the nickname "Land of Contrasts." All of this scenery lies within an area almost three times as large as the U.S. state of Texas. Mexico covers an area of 761,602 square miles (1,972,550 square kilometers).

Mexico is the southernmost country in North America and the northernmost country in Latin America. The United States borders Mexico to the north, and Guatemala and Belize lie to the south of Mexico. Three bodies of water meet Mexico's shores. The Caribbean Sea and the Gulf of Mexico lie to the east, and the Pacific Ocean washes against the west coast.

Mexico's people also make the country a land of contrasts. The nation's population of more than 100 million includes people of Spanish, native, and racially mixed backgrounds. This large population is growing quickly at an annual rate of 1.7 percent. The number of Mexicans who live in poverty also is increasing. Providing jobs, homes, and services for all citizens is a challenge for Mexico's government.

UNITED STATES

• Tijuana

• Ciudad Juárez

• Hermosillo

• Chihuahua

Gulf of California

• Batopilas

• Monterrey

Gulf of Mexico

N
W   E
S

León

Guadalajara •

Ecatepec

Mexico City ✪
•

Bay of Campeche

Caribbean Sea

PACIFIC OCEAN

• Puebla

BELIZE

• Acapulco

Gulf of Tehuantepec

GUATEMALA

Scale
Miles
0   25   50   75   100

0   50   100   150
Kilometers

Geopolitical Map of Mexico

KEY

✪ Capital

• Cities

Fast Facts about Mexico's Land

Area: 761,602 square miles (1,972,550 square kilometers)

Latitude/longitude: 23 degrees north latitude, 102 degrees west longitude

Highest elevation: Volcano Pico de Orizaba, 18,700 feet (5,700 meters)

Lowest elevation: Laguna Salada, 33 feet (10 meters) below sea level

Chapter 2

The Land, Climate, and Wildlife

Mexico has four main land regions. The Mexican Plateau covers the largest area of land. Broad mountain ranges surround the plateau. Low-lying areas line the coasts and cover the Yucatán Peninsula. Deserts stretch across northwestern Mexico. Each of these regions has a different landscape, climate, and wildlife.

Mexico's climate is mainly tropical. The summers are hot and the winters are mild. The country experiences a rainy season that lasts from June to October.

The Mexican Plateau

Central Mexico is made up of a high, flat area of land called a plateau. The plateau reaches more than 1 mile

◀ Mountains surround the Mexican Plateau.

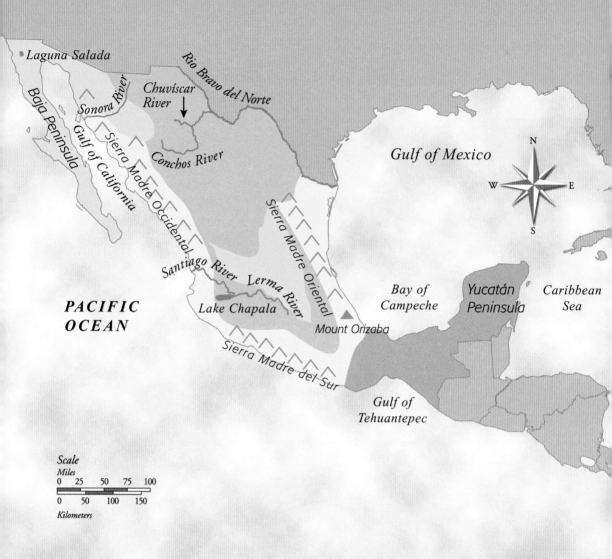

Laguna Salada

Rio Bravo del Norte

Chuvíscar River

Sonora River

Baja Peninsula

Gulf of California

Sierra Madre Occidental

Conchos River

Gulf of Mexico

N
W E
S

Santiago River

Lerma River

Sierra Madre Oriental

Bay of Campeche

Yucatán Peninsula

Caribbean Sea

PACIFIC OCEAN

Lake Chapala

Mount Orizaba

Sierra Madre del Sur

Gulf of Tehuantepec

Scale
Miles
0 25 50 75 100
0 50 100 150
Kilometers

Mexico's Land Regions and Topography

KEY

Desert Region

Mountain Region

Mexican Plateau Region

Coastal Lowlands Region

▲ Mountain

⋀ Mountain Ranges

〰 Rivers

(1.6 kilometers) above sea level in many places. The Sierra Madre del Sur mountains rise just south of the plateau.

The Mexican Plateau region contains many rivers and lakes. The Rio Bravo del Norte, a river called the Rio Grande in the United States, borders the region on the far north. Lake Chapala, Mexico's largest lake, lies near the Pacific Ocean. Lake Chapala is 50 miles (80 kilometers) long and covers more than 650 square miles (1,700 square kilometers). The Lerma River drains into Lake Chapala. The Santiago River flows from the lake's northern edge to the Pacific Ocean.

The Mexican Plateau has a mild climate. Temperatures average between 60 and 70 degrees Fahrenheit (15 and 21 degrees Celsius). Average annual rainfall on the plateau varies from 20 to 30 inches (51 to 76 centimeters).

The mild climate supports a variety of plants and animals. Crops such as corn, beans, squash, sweet potatoes, and magueys (mah-GAYS) grow well. Brush and spiny trees and shrubs also cover much of the Mexican Plateau. Deer, rabbits, iguanas, and other animals make their homes there.

The Mexican Plateau is the most populated region of the country, and some of the largest cities lie here.

Mexico City, the country's largest city, lies in the southeastern part of the region. Guadalajara in the west is the second largest city in Mexico. Monterrey lies in the northeastern part of the region, and is only slightly smaller than Guadalajara.

The Mountain Regions

Jagged mountains surround the Mexican Plateau. Volcanoes formed the Sierra Madre Oriental, the Sierra Madre Occidental, and the Sierra Madre del Sur ranges thousands of years ago. Some volcanoes in the Sierra Madre Occidental are still active. A few peaks in Mexico's mountain regions rise more than 3 miles (5 kilometers) high. The country's highest point is Mount Orizaba, a volcanic cone that is 18,700 feet (5,700 meters) tall. Located in eastern Mexico, Orizaba last erupted in 1566.

The climate in the mountains is mild at lower altitudes, from about 3,000 to 6,000 feet (900 to 1,800 meters). Here the temperature ranges between 60 and 70 degrees Fahrenheit (15 and 21 degrees Celsius), and rainfall averages between 20 and 30 inches (51 and 76 centimeters) each year. The

▼ The Sierra Madre Mountains border Mexico's Gulf Coast.

tops of the highest mountains are colder and are capped with snow year-round.

Trees and plants cover some mountain areas. Firs, pines, and oaks grow thickly on mountain slopes. Hardy plants, herbs, and low shrubs sprout on mountaintops. Grasses flourish in mountain meadows.

13

The mountains are home to a variety of wildlife. Bears, wildcats, ocelots, coyotes, and pumas hunt in the mountains. Deer, rabbits, and skunks roam the region. Birds such as turkeys, doves, mockingbirds, parakeets, and partridges live in mountain forests and grasslands. Pelicans, ducks, and sandpipers make their homes near mountain rivers and lakes.

The Coastal Lowlands

The land along the Gulf of Mexico and Pacific Ocean is mostly low and flat. The Yucatán Peninsula, which separates the Gulf of Mexico from the Caribbean Sea, also consists of lowlands. Rolling foothills, plains, sandy beaches, and wetlands cover the lowlands.

The coastal areas are tropical. The temperature is hot, reaching 72 degrees Fahrenheit (22 degrees Celsius) in winter and rising to 110 degrees Fahrenheit (43 degrees Celsius) in summer. The coasts receive large amounts of rainfall, between 60 and 200 inches (150 and 500 centimeters) each year.

Jungle vegetation covers much of the Coastal Lowlands. Forests are thick with almond, walnut, and mahogany trees. Palm, fig, and olive trees also flourish in the tropical climate. Mangrove trees thrive in southern swamp areas, and several species of orchids bloom throughout the region.

Mexico is in an earthquake zone. Earthquakes regularly rock Mexico. A disastrous earthquake struck Mexico City in 1985, killing about 10,000 people. Many victims were buried under fallen buildings.

Tsunamis can strike the coastal areas. Tsunamis are giant waves triggered by earthquakes. In 1995, a small earthquake off Mexico's Pacific shore set off a tsunami that seriously damaged beaches and homes.

The strong winds and heavy rains of hurricanes often strike Mexico's Gulf Coast. Hurricane Gilbert, one of the strongest hurricanes of the twentieth century, destroyed parts of Mexico in 1988.

▲ A 1985 earthquake that shook Mexico City crumbled buildings and killed about 10,000 people.

A wide variety of animals live in the Coastal Lowlands. Crocodiles, iguanas, snakes, and turtles crawl through the jungles. Monkeys live in the trees, while bats, macaws, and parrots fly overhead. Coastal waters support large sea snails called abalone, as well as shellfish such as lobsters, oysters, and shrimp. Anchovies, tuna, and other fish live just off Mexico's shores. Albatross, herons, and other sea birds also make their homes in the Coastal Lowlands.

The Desert Regions

North central Mexico, northwestern Mexico, and the Baja Peninsula are deserts. Much of the desert land in Mexico is rocky rather than sandy. A thin layer of topsoil covers some rocky areas. The desert landscape includes canyons and plains.

The desert regions have warm temperatures and little rainfall. Temperatures average about 75 degrees Fahrenheit (24 degrees Celsius) in winter and more than 90 degrees Fahrenheit (32 degrees Celsius) in summer. The average rainfall is less than 12 inches (30 centimeters) per year. Mexico's lowest point is 33 feet (10 meters) below sea level at Laguna Salada, near an earthquake belt in Baja, California.

The desert regions are dry year round, but they still support many plants and animals. Short grasses, boojum trees, yucca trees, cactuses, mesquite bushes, and magueys dot the region. Coyotes, gila monsters, prairie dogs, rattlesnakes, and wildcats also live there.

Most cities in the desert region were founded near water sources. Hermosillo, a town of about 400,000 people, is on the Sonora River. Ciudad Juárez, populated by about 800,000 people, lies along the Rio Bravo del Norte. Set near the Chuvíscar River, which empties into the Conchos River, Chihuahua is home to about 500,000 people.

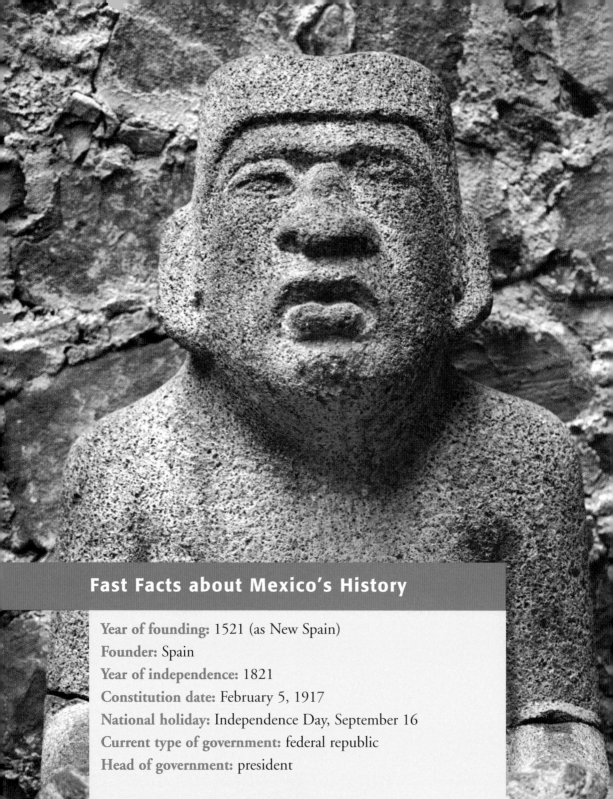

Fast Facts about Mexico's History

Year of founding: 1521 (as New Spain)

Founder: Spain

Year of independence: 1821

Constitution date: February 5, 1917

National holiday: Independence Day, September 16

Current type of government: federal republic

Head of government: president

History and Government

People have lived in the area that is now Mexico since at least 15,000 B.C. The first people to live in the region may have been hunters traveling from Asia. They moved across the land in search of small game and wild plants.

By 7000 B.C., early groups had set up farms and started to grow crops such as corn, beans, and squash. They also raised turkeys and bees. Around 3500 B.C., some people established villages. Each village had its own customs, building styles, artworks, and religious beliefs. Many cultures in Mexico rose, thrived, then died out.

Early Civilizations

One group began to build ceremonial centers along the Gulf Coast around 1200 B.C. Members shared

◄ This Olmec statue is one of many artifacts that stands as a reminder of Mexico's rich history.

large amounts of food, freeing some people from hunting and farming. These people became the Olmecs, Mexico's first great civilization.

The Olmecs built stone temples and other buildings. They carved giant heads from stone, many as large as 8 feet (2.5 meters) high and 6 feet (1.8 meters) wide. These statues may have represented Olmec gods or rulers. Olmecs also developed a calendar system. The Olmec civilization ended about 200 B.C. The people may have run out of water and food sources or may have fought among themselves or warred with another group.

The Maya civilization began as early as 2000 B.C. Members of this group settled the Yucatán Peninsula, the jungles of southern Mexico, and parts of Central America. By A.D. 300, the Mayas had built large cities with beautiful buildings, temples, and artworks. Mayan farmers raised crops such as beans, cacao, squash, and corn. The Mayas developed advanced systems of astronomy and mathematics. They recorded a written history of their culture in books called codices.

The population of the Maya civilization declined about 900, possibly due to disease or decreased food supplies. The Maya people did not disappear, however. Many Mayas still live in Mexico and Central America and speak their native Mayan languages.

▼ Ruins of the Aztecs' great city, Tenochtitlán, remain on the Mexican Plateau.

The Aztec civilization was Mexico's last great culture before European explorers arrived. The Aztecs also were called the Mexicas. The country of Mexico was named after this group.

About 1325, the Aztecs started to build a great city called Tenochtitlán in a valley on the Mexican Plateau. Built on an island in the middle of Lake Texcoco, this city had causeways that led out to surrounding lands.

The Aztecs conquered other groups in the area and forced them to pay tribute with goods and services. By 1500, the Aztecs controlled more than half of Mexico. Tenochtitlán became their political and cultural center.

The Aztecs built a huge pyramid temple to honor their most important gods. Some archeologists believe the Aztecs sacrificed humans to the gods. The Aztecs may have captured and sacrificed thousands of people from other groups.

Spanish Rule

In 1519, a Spanish explorer named Hernán Cortés arrived on the Yucatán Peninsula with about 500 European men. When Cortés saw the cities and riches of the Aztecs, he decided to conquer the area for Spain. The Aztecs' enemies helped Cortés. By 1521, Cortés had taken over Tenochtitlán, and the land was declared a colony of Spain. Cortés named this colony New Spain. He destroyed Tenochtitlán and forced the surviving Aztecs to build a Spanish city over its ruins. That city is now Mexico City, Mexico's capital.

By 1550, all of Mexico and part of the southwestern United States had come under Spanish control. The Spanish built homes and churches,

◀ This carving illustrates the friendly relationship that Hernán Cortés had with the Aztecs' enemies.

created plantations, mined gold and silver, started industries, and introduced new crops and animals. Spanish priests converted native people to the Catholic religion. The Catholic Church in New Spain became rich and powerful.

Spanish rulers set up two classes in New Spain. A small, powerful class consisted of a few Spanish leaders who controlled almost all of New Spain's wealth. Native people, called indígenas, made up the

This statue stands as a monument to heroes of the War of Independence first led by Miguel Hidalgo y Costilla.

larger class. They became subjects of the Spaniards. Millions of indígenas died from European diseases, such as measles, smallpox, and typhus.

Two other ethnic groups arose during the Spanish rule of New Spain. Many Spanish men had children with indígena women. Over time, people who had a mixed Spanish and indígena background became known as mestizos (meh-STEE-zohs). People born in New Spain to Spanish parents made up a group called criollos. Both criollos and mestizos were part of a middle class between the Spaniards and indígenas.

By the beginning of the 1800s, many mestizos, indígenas, and criollos had become dissatisfied with the ruling of New Spain. Many criollos were jealous of the power that Spaniards held. Mestizos and indígenas were tired of high taxes and wanted more freedom. These Mexicans wanted their independence from Spain.

Independence

The Mexicans' first rebellion against Spain occurred in 1810. Miguel Hidalgo y Costilla called for the end of slavery, the end of unfair taxes, and the end of Spanish rule in New Spain. He and his followers entered Guanajuato, a colonial mining town populated mainly by rich Spaniards. They killed many Spanish people who lived there. The Spanish government then killed Hidalgo.

Hidalgo's rebellion ended, but another rebellion began. Led by José María Morelos y Pavón, troops took control of parts of southern Mexico. Morelos formally called for independence at the Congress of Chilpancingo in 1813. General Agustín de Iturbide, a criollo, led Spanish forces that defeated Morelos and his troops later that year. After the death of Morelos, Vincente Guerrero led the rebel forces.

The Spanish government began using a new constitution in 1820. Some Mexicans, including Iturbide, did not agree with these laws. Iturbide became a spokesperson for rich criollos who wanted to break away from Spain and rule themselves. Guerrero and Iturbide met and agreed to bring their forces together, forcing Spain to accept the independent Mexican Empire in 1821.

The first years of independence were difficult for Mexico. Leaders needed to write a constitution, but they disagreed on a type of government. Some people wanted a strong central government, while others wanted the states to have more power. These two groups struggled for control of the new Mexican republic.

During the next 40 years, many presidents and governments came and went in Mexico. Iturbide became emperor of the Mexican Empire in 1821, but the military overthrew him in 1823. The military then declared Mexico a democratic republic with Guadelupe Victoria as president. Guerrero became president in 1829, but he was killed in another military revolt. Instability troubled the new country.

Benito Juárez and Porfirio Díaz

Benito Juárez became president of Mexico in 1861. He took power away from the Catholic Church,

giving land back to indígenas. Juárez started to reform
Mexico's educational system and worked to improve
the economy. With the help of foreign governments,
Mexico built railways, roads, and telegraph networks.
During all but a few years, Juárez was president until
his death in 1872.

After Juárez died, Mexicans elected Porfirio Díaz as
president. He became a dictator, ruling Mexico from
1877 to 1911. Díaz continued to improve Mexico. He
invited foreign businesses to build railways and

streetcars, to lay electric lines, to develop industry, to improve ports, and to mine minerals. Díaz's policies created new wealth in Mexico. But only a few people, including foreigners, earned money. Mexican workers were paid almost nothing.

The 1900s

In 1910, Mexicans rose up against Díaz's government. They wanted land reform, more schools, civil liberties, and better working conditions. Emiliano Zapata led one group of soldiers. Pancho Villa led another. Many people died during the revolution. This conflict forced Díaz from the presidency in 1911.

After the revolution, Mexico went through another difficult time. One leader after another seized power and was overthrown. Leaders disagreed on how to run Mexico and pay its debts. After many discussions, the country adopted its present constitution in 1917.

The Institutional Revolutionary Party (PRI) came into power in 1929. This political party stabilized Mexico's government. The government then built new schools and improved education. It broke up some large ranches and gave land to poor people.

World War II

World events became important to Mexico in the mid-1900s. In 1939, German dictator Adolf Hitler invaded Poland, beginning World War II (1939–1945). Mexico did not send troops into the war until 1942, but the country did supply the United States and other countries with needed materials. Many Mexicans moved to the United States to work in agriculture. The two countries started to create a good relationship.

After World War II, Mexico's economy and population grew. From the 1950s to the 1970s, Mexico strengthened its industry. But corrupt government officials took much of the money for themselves. Most Mexicans remained poor. The number of Mexicans who lived in poverty also began to increase. The economy could not keep up with the fast-growing population.

Modern Mexico

Mexico experienced difficulties in the 1980s. Oil prices dropped, and the government had less money to repay foreign loans. The United States helped Mexico pay some of its debts. In 1985, an earthquake destroyed parts of Mexico City. About 10,000 people died, and many buildings collapsed. Many Mexicans criticized the government for being slow to rebuild the city.

In 1992, Canada, Mexico, and the United States signed the North American Free Trade Agreement (NAFTA). This pact allowed Mexico to trade more easily with Canada and the United States. Some Mexicans believe NAFTA helped the economy improve.

Some indígenas did not support NAFTA. They did not want the government to use their land to harvest timber and crops that would be exported to other countries. They wanted the government to give the land to poor people. In 1994, these people began a rebellion. The government made a truce with the rebels, but fighting still breaks out sometimes.

▲ Many Mexicans struggle to earn a living. These women make and sell baskets to earn money.

Mexico's unstable economy made many foreign businesses and governments unwilling to invest money in Mexico. Some foreign-owned businesses even left the country. Millions of people lost their jobs, and Mexico's economic troubles worsened. But Mexicans remain hopeful that NAFTA will lead to new industry and jobs in Mexico.

Vincente Fox (left) became president of Mexico in December 2000. Here, he meets with U.S. president George W. Bush.

A Change in Leadership

In Mexico, the president is very powerful. The president appoints many government leaders. From 1929 to 2000, each president was a member of the PRI. Many people believe that the PRI has done little to help most Mexicans. For this reason, many Mexicans now support other political parties. The National Action Party (PAN), the Party of the Democratic Revolution, and other parties have gained power in Mexico. Many Mexicans believe that the work of these new parties may lead to a change for the better.

In July 2000, Vincente Fox won the presidential election. Fox, a member of the PAN, defeated the PRI candidate. This defeat marked the end of the PRI's 71-year dominance in Mexican politics. Fox took office in December 2000. He promised to improve the Mexican government.

Today's Government

Mexico is a federal republic divided into 31 states and a Federal District. A president and a legislature govern the country. The president is elected to a six-year term and cannot be re-elected. The legislature is a group that makes new laws.

Mexico's legislature consists of two houses. One house is the Senate, which has 128 members. Four senators are elected from each state and from the Federal District. The senators serve six-year terms. The other house is the Chamber of Deputies, which contains 500 members elected from around the country. The deputies serve three-year terms. Senators and deputies cannot serve two terms in a row.

The Supreme Court of Justice heads Mexico's judicial system. Twenty-one judges serve on this court. Mexico also has many circuit courts and district courts to deal with local matters.

Fast Facts about Mexico's Economy

Major natural resources/minerals: timber, copper, gold, petroleum, lead, natural gas, silver, zinc

Major agricultural products: fruits, vegetables, cacao, coffee, grains, cotton, soybeans, sugarcane, dairy products, beef, poultry

Major types of manufactured products: textiles, glass, leather goods, machinery and electronic equipment, motor vehicles, paper, pottery, turpentine

Major exports: oil and oil products, silver, cotton, coffee, motor vehicles, engines, computer and electrical parts

Major imports: grains, paper, steel products, electrical equipment, agricultural machinery, automobile and aircraft parts

Mexico's Economy

Mexico's labor force has more than 39 million people. Only about 3 percent of Mexicans are unemployed, but another 20 percent work in jobs that pay too little money to provide basic needs.

The standard of living varies greatly among Mexicans. A small group of very wealthy citizens owns or controls most industries in Mexico. Other people are professionals who make a comfortable living. This group is made up of office workers, health care workers, engineers, lawyers, scientists, and teachers. The vast majority of Mexicans are poor.

Mexico's unemployment rate is steadily increasing because jobs are scarce. As a result, the number of Mexicans who live in poverty is rising quickly. Mexico's government is working to provide a better economic future for its people.

◀ A rancher herds cattle on Mexico's plains. Many Mexicans live in areas where they raise a variety of crops and animals.

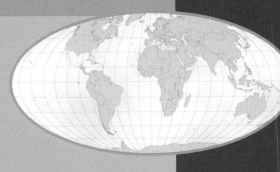

Mexico's Industries and Natural Resources

KEY

- Coffee
- **G** Gold
- Iron ore
- Manufacturing
- Rice
- Soybeans
- Wheat

Scale
Miles
0   25   50   75   100

0   50   100   150
Kilometers

Agriculture, Fishing, and Forestry

The richest farmland in Mexico lies along the southern coasts. Farmers have built large irrigation systems to bring water to dry northern Mexico.

Mexico has a system of farms called ejidos (eh-HEED-ohs). Each ejido is owned by a group of people who work the land together. Indígenas and mestizos run most ejidos. In recent years, many workers have left ejidos to look for better-paying jobs in cities.

Mexico produces a wide variety of crops. Grains grown include barley, oats, wheat, and rice. Mangoes, oranges, bananas, papayas, and other fruits flourish throughout the country. Vegetables, such as beans, corn, chickpeas, and squash, also come from Mexico. Much of the world's coffee, cotton, peanuts, and vanilla are grown in the country. Mexico uses some produce for its own needs and exports the rest.

Farmers raise livestock such as cattle, chickens, goats, hogs, and sheep. Farmers raise some animals for their meat and others to make dairy products such as butter and cheese. Many farmers keep horses and mules to help with farmwork.

Mexico has a commercial fishing fleet that operates in the Gulf of California and in the Gulf of Mexico. Fishers catch anchovies, sardines, tuna, abalone, lobsters, and shrimp. Some seafood is sold in Mexico, and the rest is exported.

Forests cover about one-fourth of Mexico. The country's valuable trees include ebony, mahogany, pine, sapodilla, rosewood, and walnut. Chicle, which comes from the sapodilla tree, is used to make gum. Mexico produces many forestry products, including lumber, paper, and turpentine. Workers also harvest resins, which are ingredients in paints and varnishes.

Energy and Mining

Mexico uses fossil fuels, such as oil and natural gas, to produce about 80 percent of the country's electricity. The rushing waters of the country's large rivers create hydroelectric power. Nuclear power, solar power, and wind power also produce electricity for the country.

Mexico's mountains are rich in minerals. Silver, lead, copper, gold, salt, and zinc are the country's chief minerals. Mexico is the world's leading silver producer, digging up about one-sixth of the world's annual silver supply. Miners also dig up coal and iron ore. Some coal is used to produce electricity.

Oil is one of Mexico's most valuable resources. The government runs much of the country's oil industry. About 40 percent of the government's money comes from oil sales. Mexico exports about half of the oil it produces, supplying many countries with this resource.

Manufacturing and Transportation

Most of Mexico's industries are in Mexico City, Monterrey, and Guadalajara. Factories in these areas produce automobiles, iron and steel products, and electrical machinery. Workers make cement, glass, and paper in factories. Artisans craft pottery, leather goods, and textiles. Mexico also has cotton mills, meatpacking plants, tobacco-processing plants, breweries, and sugar refineries.

About 4,500 foreign-owned factories operate near the Mexican-U.S. border. These businesses import materials and use them to make products such as clothing, medical supplies, motor vehicles, and toys. The products then are exported back to the United States and to other countries. These factories provide many jobs for Mexicans. It is often less expensive for foreign companies to hire Mexican workers than to hire workers in their own countries.

Mexico has a good transportation system. Common modes of transportation include a subway system called the "Metro," trains, cars, buses, and airplanes. Mexico City, Monterrey, and Guadalajara all have international airports. Trucks move the majority of goods within Mexico, where highways link most areas of the country.

Service Industries

About 50 percent of Mexican workers are employed in service industries. Service industry employees include teachers, store clerks, bank tellers, and accountants.

Tourism is the country's largest source of employment. This service industry creates many jobs in hotels and restaurants. More than 6 million people visit Mexico each year to enjoy the country's beaches, mountains, and to tour ancient ruins.

Mexico's Money

Mexico's unit of currency is the peso, which is available in coins and bills. One peso equals 100 centavos. Exchange rates change every day. In the early 2000s, about 9.20 pesos equaled 1 U.S. dollar, and about 5.98 pesos equaled 1 Canadian dollar.

5 peso coin

100 peso coin

100 peso bill

5 centavos coin

10 centavos coin

100 peso coin

2000 peso bill

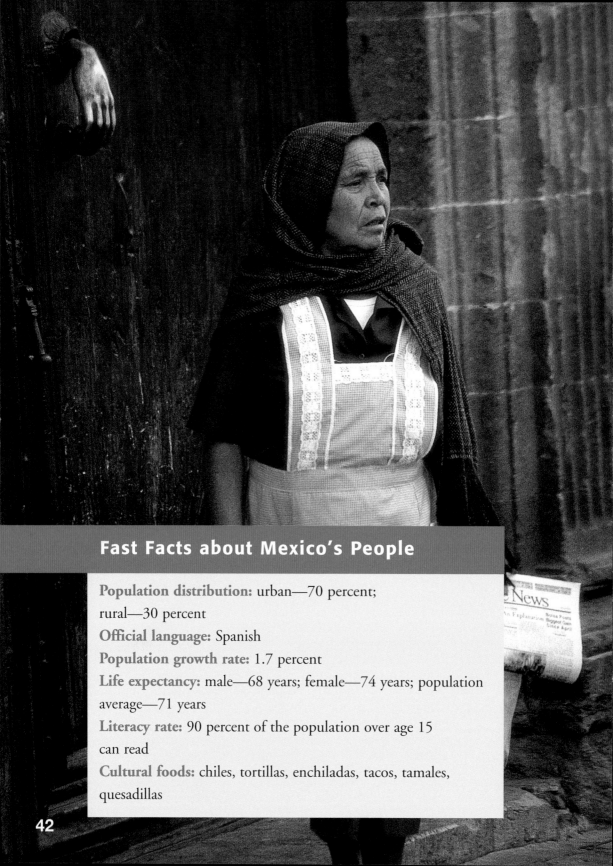

Fast Facts about Mexico's People

Population distribution: urban—70 percent;
rural—30 percent

Official language: Spanish

Population growth rate: 1.7 percent

Life expectancy: male—68 years; female—74 years; population
average—71 years

Literacy rate: 90 percent of the population over age 15
can read

Cultural foods: chiles, tortillas, enchiladas, tacos, tamales,
quesadillas

People, Culture, and Daily Life

Mexico has more than 100 million people who belong to many ethnic groups. Mestizos are the largest ethnic group, making up 60 percent of the population. About 30 percent of Mexicans are indígenas. People of mixed ethnic backgrounds make up about 9 percent of Mexico's population. People with other ethnic backgrounds, such as Chinese or African, compose about 1 percent of the country's population.

The indígenas of Mexico belong to at least 56 different native groups. Many are poor and live in rural areas where they farm or raise cattle for food. Unable to make a living on farms, some indígenas move to cities to find jobs in factories or stores. Indígenas generally receive less education and poorer health care than other Mexican citizens do. They have fought for equal rights for many years.

◀ Some indígenas move to cities to work in factories or stores.

Most Mexicans speak Spanish, the official language of Mexico. Indígenas usually speak their native tongue as well as Spanish. One-tenth of Mexico's indígenas speak only their native language. At least 50 native languages exist in Mexico, including Maya, Nahuatl, and Zapotec.

Living in Mexico

About 70 percent of Mexicans live in urban areas. These cities have office buildings, government buildings, churches, factories, and schools. City dwellers shop, eat in restaurants, visit museums, and go to the movies. Mexican cities often have a town square where people meet and hold celebrations. Cities also have an outdoor marketplace where people sell fruits, vegetables, meat, clothing, flowers, pottery, and other goods.

In the middle-class and wealthy neighborhoods of cities, people live in large, comfortable homes. Each house has a central patio with flowers, grass, and trees. Some city dwellers live in tall apartment buildings. Poor Mexicans often live in slums that surround cities. The homes in these crowded neighborhoods are temporary shelters made of scrap wood, cardboard, tin, and plastic.

About 30 percent of Mexicans live in rural areas. Some live and work on large estates called haciendas

▼ Most Mexicans live in urban areas such as Mexico City.

that belong to wealthy landowners. Others find jobs on ejidos. Rural residents live in houses made of adobe, a type of sun-dried clay brick. Some houses are built from poles, cornstalks, and mud. Homes in the countryside usually have one or two small rooms and

Learn to Speak Spanish

Spanish has five basic vowel sounds.

A is pronounced as a in far.   E is pronounced as ay in pay.   I is pronounced as ee in need.

O is pronounced as o in toe. U is pronounced as oo in boo.

Basic Phrases

hello	hola	(OH-lah)
good-bye	adios	(ah-dee-OHS)
please	por favor	(PORE fah-VORE)
thank you	gracias	(GRAH-syahs)
Do you speak English?	¿Habla inglés?	(AH-blah een-GLEHS)

◄ These Mexican students attend a church-run school, where they learn Spanish and English.

very little furniture. These huts often have no electricity, telephones, or plumbing.

Education and Religion

Mexico provides free education for children between the ages of 6 and 18. Most Mexican schools are run by the national government. A few are church-run schools. In both types of schools, the government chooses the curriculum, and students study subjects such as language, science, math, and history. Most children go to school for at least five years to learn to read and write. Mexico's literacy rate is almost 90 percent.

There are about fifty universities in Mexico, as well as hundreds of professional, vocational, and military colleges. Most Mexicans believe a college degree is important for economic and social success. But fewer than 10 percent of Mexicans receive a higher education.

About 89 percent of Mexico's population is Roman Catholic. Many Mexicans mix their Catholic beliefs with ancient native beliefs. Six percent of Mexico's population is Protestant. Small numbers of Jews, Mormons, and Mennonites also live in Mexico.

Sports and Recreation

The most popular sport in Mexico is soccer, or fútbol. Mexicans enjoy playing soccer and watching their national soccer team compete. Other popular sports to play and watch are baseball and basketball. Bullfighting is the national sport, and many Mexicans also like to watch rodeos.

Mexicans enjoy many of the same pastimes as people do in Canada and the United States. They watch movies, attend concerts, and watch television. Many people like to travel around Mexico and around the world.

Music, Literature, and Art

Mexicans listen to many kinds of music. Mariachi bands, which feature guitars, trumpets, and violins, are very popular. The accordion is the main instrument in a type of music called norteña (nor-TEHN-ya), from northern Mexico. This music mixes polkas, waltzes, Mexican cowboy songs, and ballads. Mexicans also listen to traditional native and folk music. Folk instruments include reed flutes, gourd rattles, and drums. Mexican radio and TV stations feature more modern music, such as rock, reggae, and rap.

▼ Bullfighting is Mexico's national sport. A matador, or bullfighter, prepares for the bull's next charge.

Mexico has a rich tradition of literature. The poetry of a seventeenth-century nun named Sor Juana Inés de la Cruz is considered to be among the finest ever written in Spanish. The writings of modern authors such as Octavio Paz and Laura Esquival are read in many countries.

▲ Some Mexican artisans make pottery pieces that are sold in Mexican stores and exported to other countries.

Artisans throughout Mexico craft a variety of handmade items. Folk artists make pottery, glass, jewelry, and leather work. Many craftspeople weave textiles, clothing, mats, and baskets. Hats, wood carvings, paintings, and furniture are other popular arts.

Twentieth-century Mexican painters Diego Rivera and Frida Kahlo are known all over the world. Rivera painted large murals showing historical events. Kahlo's paintings are mixtures of Mexican folk art, self-portraits, fantasy, and scenes from her life.

Make Mexican Chocolate

Cacao beans, used to make chocolate, have grown in Mexico for thousands of years. The ancient Mayas and Aztecs made a drink from cacao beans and water. They also used cacao beans as currency. Today, chocolate is still a popular drink in Mexico.

Mexican chocolate is different from other chocolates. It is combined with cinnamon and vanilla for a special taste. You can find Mexican chocolate in the Mexican foods section of most grocery stores. Most Mexican chocolate is sold in the form of solid round discs.

What You Need

3 ounces (90 grams) Mexican chocolate

3 cups milk (750 ml)

medium saucepan

liquid measuring cup

electric mixer or egg beaters

cups for serving

What You Do

1. Place the Mexican chocolate and milk in a medium saucepan. Heat for 15 minutes over medium heat, allowing the chocolate to melt. Stir every two minutes.
2. Using an electric mixer or egg beaters, beat the milk and chocolate mixture in the saucepan for one minute.
3. Allow the mixture to settle. Heat for five minutes longer. Beat mixture again for one minute. The mixture will be frothy.
4. Pour the hot chocolate drink into cups and serve immediately.

Makes three servings

▼ For celebrations, many Mexicans wear traditional clothing such as sombrero hats and brightly colored dresses.

Food and Clothing

Mexican meals usually feature dishes prepared with beans, corn, and chili peppers. Chili rellenos, or stuffed chili peppers, are a favorite. Mexicans also enjoy corn chowder called pozole and stuffed corn husks called tamales. Flat cornmeal breads known as tortillas are served with most meals. Chicken with mole, a spicy sauce, is a popular main dish.

A traditional Mexican drink is pulque (POOL-keh), made from the maguey plant. Ancient Indians used pulque in healing rituals. The most famous Mexican drink is tequila, a liquor made from the agave plant. Soft drinks and fruit juices also are popular in Mexico.

Most Mexicans wear clothing similar to that of other North Americans. Some indígenas in rural regions wear traditional clothing such as woolen skirts, thick ponchos, suits called charros, and woven serapes (seh-RAH-pehs), or shawls. Other traditional Mexican clothing includes wide-brimmed hats called sombreros, loose-fitting dresses, embroidered cotton shirts, and brightly colored belts.

Holidays and Celebrations

Most Mexican holidays are related to religious celebrations. Catholics and other Christians celebrate Easter and Christmas. During the celebration of Las Posadas, people march in candlelight processions. They celebrate Joseph and Mary's search for shelter in Bethlehem on the night Jesus was born.

Catholic observances include Saint John the Baptist Day, the Feast of the Assumption of the Virgin Mary, and the Feast of the Virgin of Guadalupe, Mexico's patron saint. Mexicans also celebrate many saints' days, honoring a town's patron saint with parades and festivals.

Some holidays are a mixture of Catholic and ancient beliefs. El Día de los Muertos, or Day of the Dead, occurs on November 2. This holiday celebrates the lives of people who have died. Families decorate graves with flowers and light candles in honor of loved ones.

Mexicans also celebrate many national holidays. They include New Year's Day, the birthday of Benito Juárez, and Constitution Day. September 16 is Mexican Independence Day, marking the anniversary of the first public call to fight for freedom from Spain.

▼ Mexico's many festivals include singing and dancing to traditional Mexican music performed by mariachi bands.

▲ Aztec temples still stand strong centuries after their construction.

Mexico's National Symbols

◀ **Mexico's Flag**

The Mexican flag was adopted in 1821, when Mexico gained its independence from Spain. The flag has three vertical stripes of green, white, and red. Green stands for independence, white represents religion, and red stands for unity. Mexico's coat of arms is in the center of the flag.

◀ **Mexico's Coat of Arms**

Mexico's coat of arms shows an eagle perched on a cactus holding a snake in its beak. This symbol comes from the Aztecs, who ruled Mexico hundreds of years ago. According to legend, a god told the Aztecs to build their capital, Tenochtitlán, where they saw an eagle on a cactus eating a snake. Mexico City now stands on that site.

Other National Symbols

National Anthem: "Himno Nacional de México"
National Bird: crested caracara
National Flower: dahlia
National Tree: Mexican cypress

Timeline

1200 B.C. to 200 B.C.
The Olmec civilization flourishes.

1325 to 1521
The Aztec civilization controls more of Mexico.

1821
Mexico becomes independent from Spain.

1877 to 1911
Porfirio Díaz is president of Mexico; many Mexicans become unhappy with the government.

B.C.   A.D.   1000   1500   1800   1900

Before 15,000 B.C.
The first people arrive in Mexico; early groups lived as nomads.

A.D. 300 to 900
The Maya civilization thrives.

1521
Hernán Cortés conquers the Aztecs and makes Mexico a colony of Spain.

1861 to 1872
During all except a few years, Benito Juárez is president of Mexico; he starts to modernize the country.

1917
Mexico adopts it present constitution.

1942
Mexico sends troops to fight in World War II (1939–1945).

1994
The Zapatista rebellion begins.

1910   **1940**   **1980**   **2000**

1910 to 1911
Emiliano Zapata and Pancho Villa lead Mexicans during the Mexican revolution.

1929
The political party now called the PRI comes into power in Mexico.

1985
An earthquake destroys parts of Mexico City.

2000
Vicente Fox of the PAN party is elected president of Mexico.

Words to Know

archeologist (ar-kee-OL-uh-jist)—a scientist who studies the remains of the lives and cultures of ancient people

artisan (AR-tih-sahn)—someone skilled at a craft

astronomy (uh-STRON-uh-mee)—the study of the stars, planets, and space

causeway (KAWZ-way)—a raised road built across water or low ground

civilization (siv-i-luh-ZAY-shuhn)—a highly developed and organized society

codices (COH-duh-sees)—ancient books

ejidos (eh-HEED-ohs)—a system of farms in Mexico

hydroelectric power (hye-droh-i-LEK-trik POU-ur)—electricity made from energy produced by running water; hydroelectric power plants often are built on dams.

maquey (mah-GAY)—a plant that has spiny leaves

nuclear power (NOO-klee-ur POU-ur)—power created by splitting atoms

ocelot (AH-suh-loht)—a wildcat that has a yellow or gray coat with black stripes

tsunami (tsoo-NAH-mee)—a destructive wave caused by an earthquake

To Learn More

Alcraft, Rob. *Mexico.* A Visit to. Des Plaines, Ill.: Heinemann Library, 1999.

Ardagh, Philip. *Aztecs.* History Detectives. New York: Peter Bedrick Books, 2000.

Cory, Steve. *Daily Life in Ancient and Modern Mexico City.* Cities through Time. Minneapolis: Runestone Press, 1999.

Furlong, Kate A. *Mexico.* The Countries. Edina, Minn.: Abdo, 2000.

Goodwin, William. *Mexico.* Modern Nations of the World. San Diego: Lucent Books, 1999.

Rummel, Jack. *Mexico.* Major World Nations. Philadelphia: Chelsea House, 1999.

Useful Addresses

The Embassy of Mexico

1911 Pennsylvania Avenue NW

Washington, DC 20006

Mexican Consulate

199 Bay Street

Suite 4440

Commerce Court West

Toronto, ON M5L 1E9

Canada

Internet Sites

Ancient Maya

http://www.penncharter.com/Student/maya/index.html

Discover the world of the ancient Mayas.

CIA—World Factbook: Mexico

http://www.cia.gov/cia/publications/factbook/geos/mx.html

Statistics and basic information on Mexico

Culture and Society of Mexico

http://www.public.iastate.edu/~rjsalvad/scmfaq/scmfaq.html

Learn about customs and traditions of Mexico's culture.

Embassy of Mexico in Canada

http://www.embamexcan.com

Government site including a wide range of information

▲ The sandy beaches that line Mexico's coasts attract many tourists.

Index